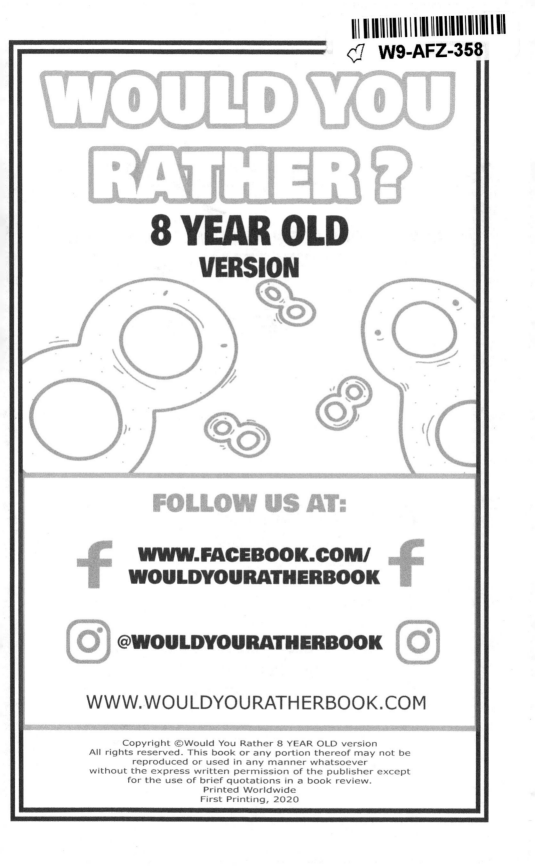

WOULD YOU RATHER ?

8 YEAR OLD
VERSION

FOLLOW US AT:

**WWW.FACEBOOK.COM/
WOULDYOURATHERBOOK**

@WOULDYOURATHERBOOK

WWW.WOULDYOURATHERBOOK.COM

COME
JOIN OUR GROUP

**GET A BONUS PDF PACKED WITH HILARIOUS
JOKES, AND THINGS TO MAKE YOU SMILE!**

GO TO:

shorturl.at/cdLRT

■ *Get a Bonus fun PDF* (filled
with jokes, and fun would you rather
questions)

■ *Get entered into our monthly
competition to win a $100 Amazon
gift card*

■ *Hear about our up and coming
new books*

HOW TO PLAY?

You can play to win or play for fun, the choice is yours!

1. Player 1 asks player 2 to either choose questions **A** or **B**.

2. Then player 1 reads out the chosen questions.

3. Player 2 decides on an answer to their dilemma, and either memorize their answer or notes it down.

4. Player 1 has to guess player 2's answer. If they guess correctly they win a point, if not player 2 wins a point.

5. Take turns asking the questions, **the first to 7 points wins.**

(Note: It can be fun to do funny voices or make silly faces)

REMEMBER
Do **NOT** ATTEMPT TO DO ANY OF THE SCENARIOS IN THIS BOOK, THEY ARE ONLY MEANT FOR FUN!

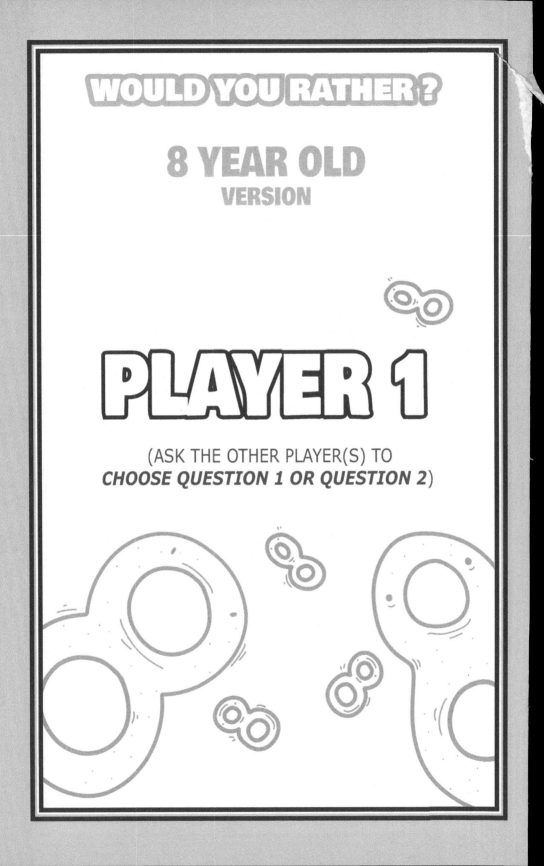

WOULD YOU RATHER?

8 YEAR OLD
VERSION

PLAYER 1

(ASK THE OTHER PLAYER(S) TO
CHOOSE QUESTION 1 OR QUESTION 2)

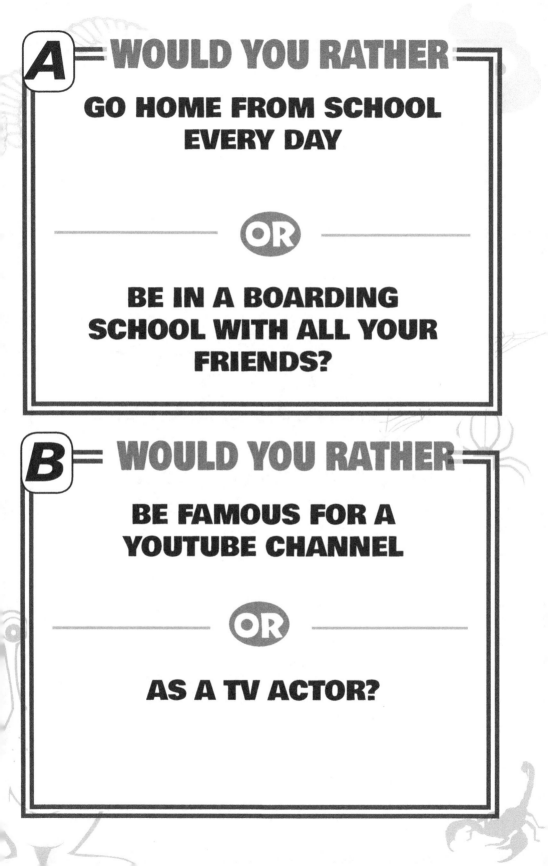

WOULD YOU RATHER ?

8 YEAR OLD
VERSION

PLAYER 2

(ASK THE OTHER PLAYER(S) TO
CHOOSE QUESTION 1 OR QUESTION 2)

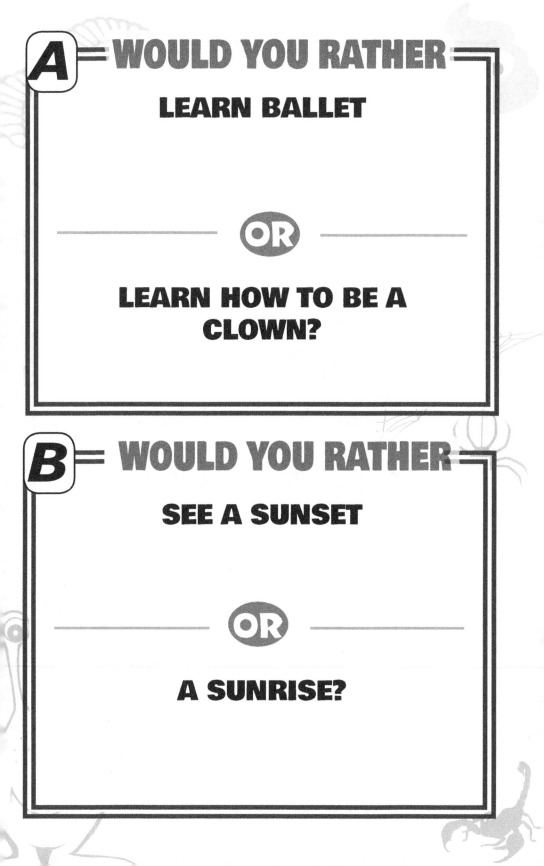

A WOULD YOU RATHER

LEARN BALLET

OR

LEARN HOW TO BE A CLOWN?

B WOULD YOU RATHER

SEE A SUNSET

OR

A SUNRISE?

A — WOULD YOU RATHER

FLY IN A STUNT PLANE

OR

A HOT AIR BALLOON?

B — WOULD YOU RATHER

WIN A QUIZ

OR

WIN A DEBATE?

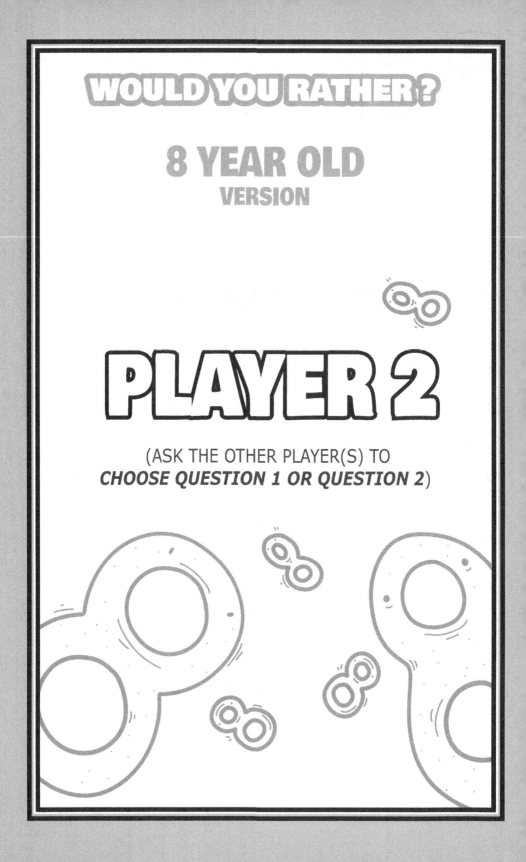

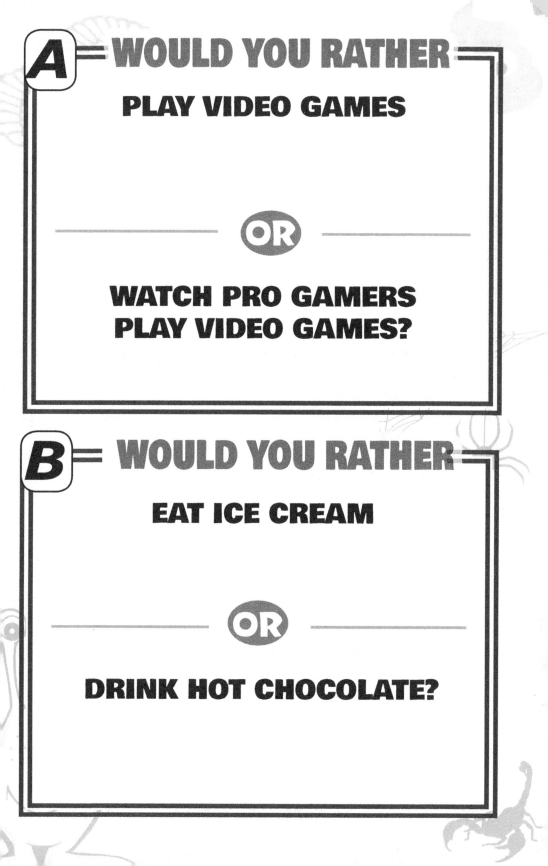

A | WOULD YOU RATHER

PLAY VIDEO GAMES

OR

WATCH PRO GAMERS PLAY VIDEO GAMES?

B | WOULD YOU RATHER

EAT ICE CREAM

OR

DRINK HOT CHOCOLATE?

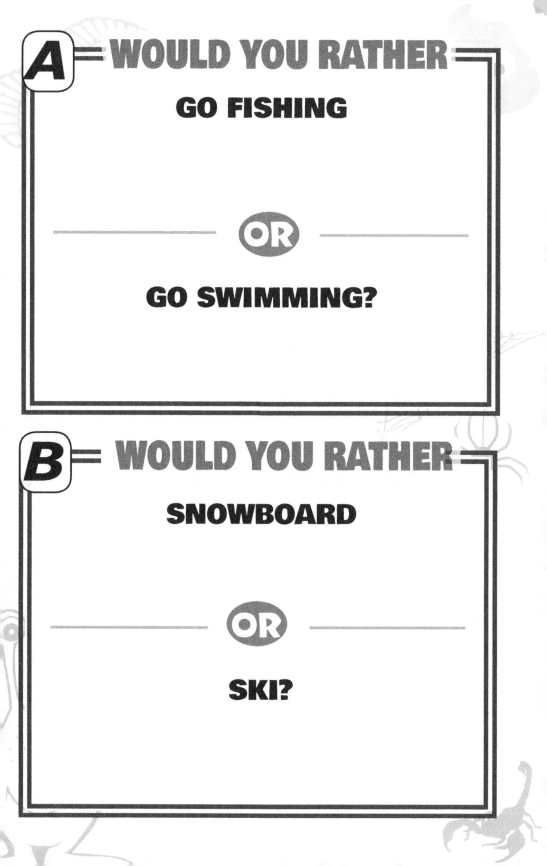

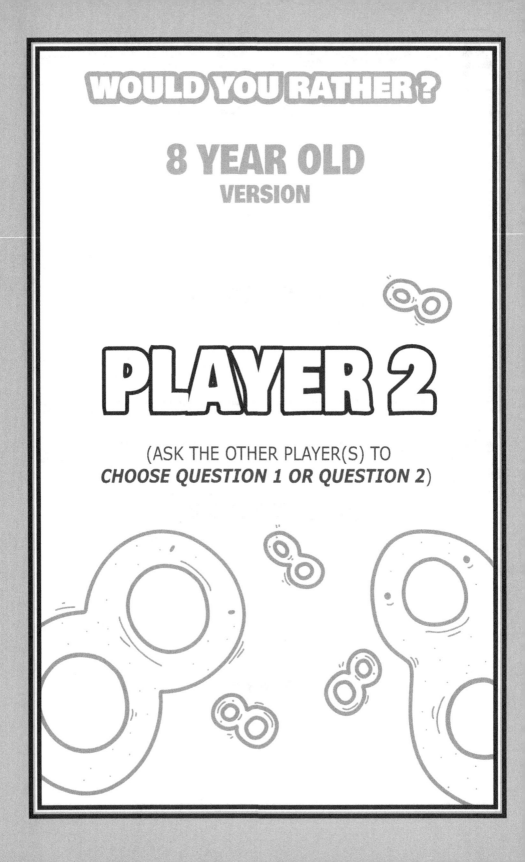

WOULD YOU RATHER

MISS A DAY AT SCHOOL AND HAVE TO SPEND ALL DAY IN BED

OR

GO TO SCHOOL AND PLAY IN THE SUNSHINE AFTERWARD?

WOULD YOU RATHER

HAVE THE CHANCE TO ICE SKATE

OR

ROLLER SKATE?

WOULD YOU RATHER ?

8 YEAR OLD
VERSION

PLAYER 1

(ASK THE OTHER PLAYER(S) TO
CHOOSE QUESTION 1 OR QUESTION 2)

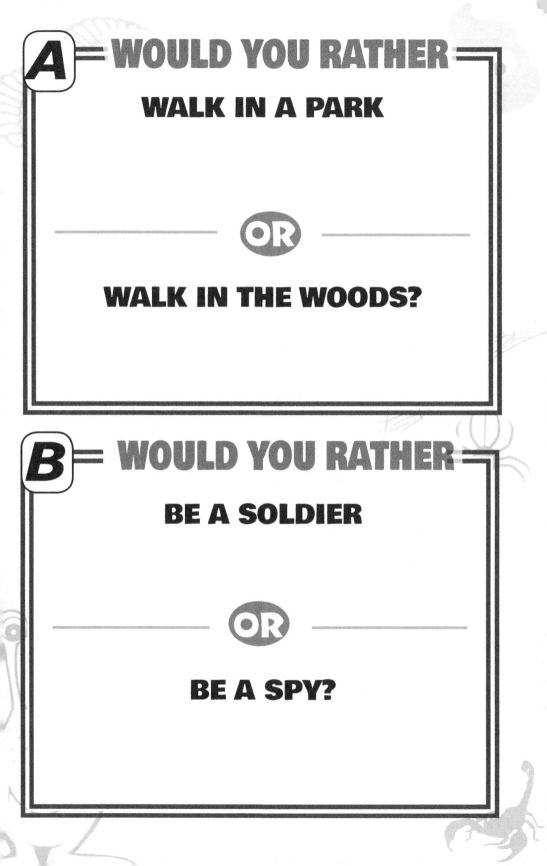

A — WOULD YOU RATHER

WALK IN A PARK

OR

WALK IN THE WOODS?

B — WOULD YOU RATHER

BE A SOLDIER

OR

BE A SPY?

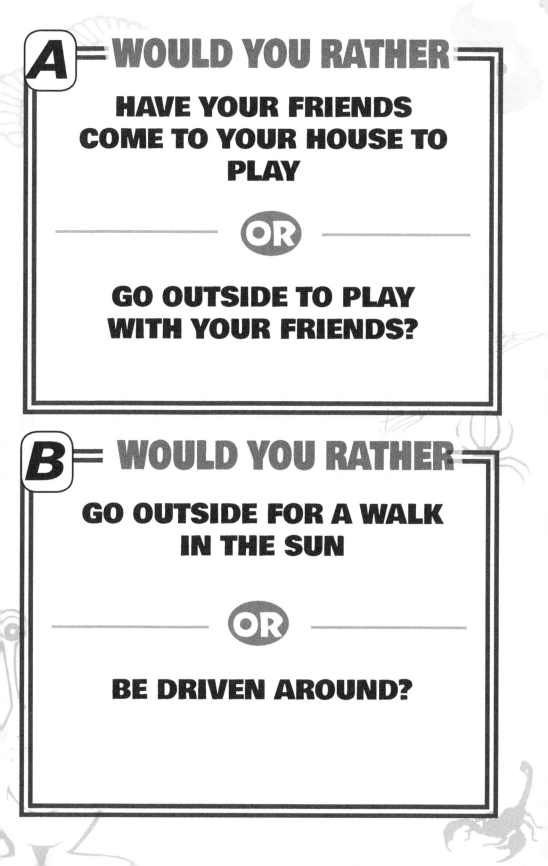

A ═ **WOULD YOU RATHER** ═

HAVE YOUR FRIENDS COME TO YOUR HOUSE TO PLAY

OR

GO OUTSIDE TO PLAY WITH YOUR FRIENDS?

B ═ **WOULD YOU RATHER** ═

GO OUTSIDE FOR A WALK IN THE SUN

OR

BE DRIVEN AROUND?

WOULD YOU RATHER ?

8 YEAR OLD
VERSION

PLAYER 1

(ASK THE OTHER PLAYER(S) TO
CHOOSE QUESTION 1 OR QUESTION 2)

A = WOULD YOU RATHER =

GO SWIMMING

OR

SUNBATHE?

B = WOULD YOU RATHER =

BE ABLE TO HAVE A PET LION

OR

A PET CHIMP?

WOULD YOU RATHER ?

8 YEAR OLD
VERSION

PLAYER 2

(ASK THE OTHER PLAYER(S) TO
CHOOSE QUESTION 1 OR QUESTION 2)

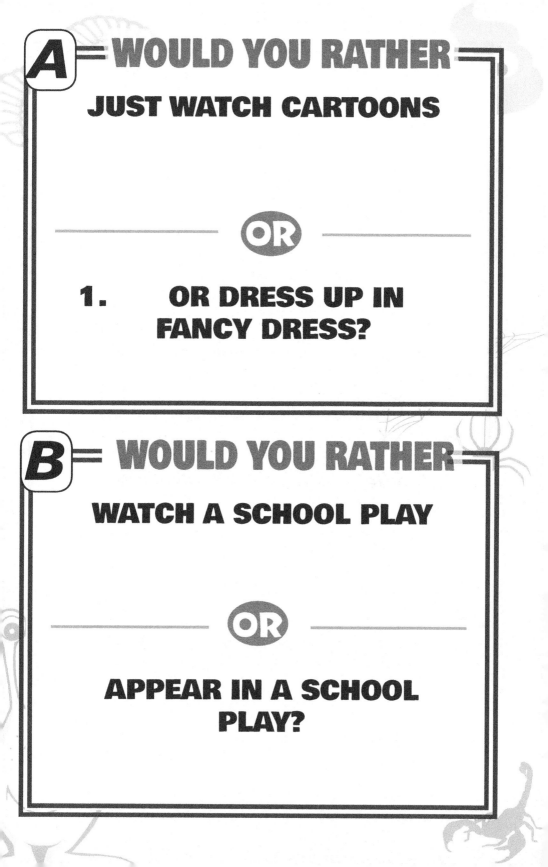

A — WOULD YOU RATHER

JUST WATCH CARTOONS

OR

1. OR DRESS UP IN FANCY DRESS?

B — WOULD YOU RATHER

WATCH A SCHOOL PLAY

OR

APPEAR IN A SCHOOL PLAY?

A. WOULD YOU RATHER

GO TRICK OR TREATING

OR

GO TO A FIREWORKS DISPLAY?

B. WOULD YOU RATHER

ONLY EAT BREAKFAST

OR

ONLY EAT LUNCH?

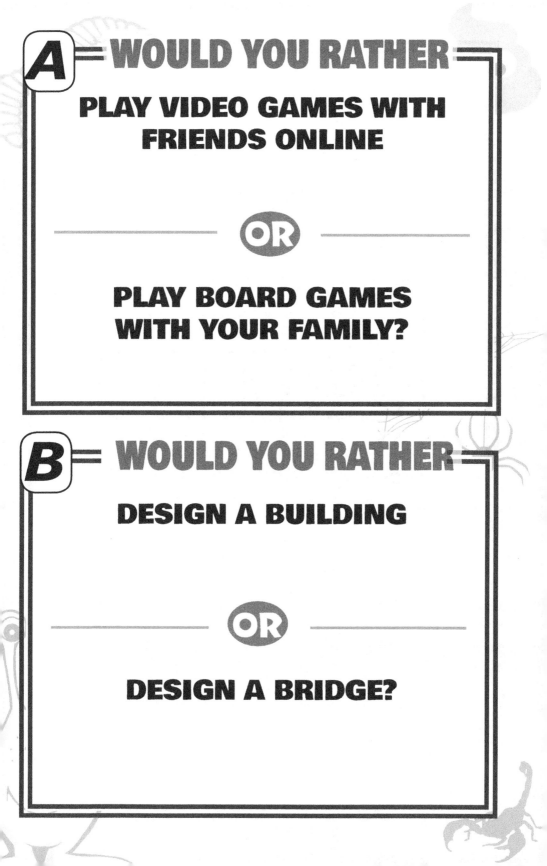

A = WOULD YOU RATHER

PLAY VIDEO GAMES WITH FRIENDS ONLINE

OR

PLAY BOARD GAMES WITH YOUR FAMILY?

B = WOULD YOU RATHER

DESIGN A BUILDING

OR

DESIGN A BRIDGE?

WOULD YOU RATHER?

8 YEAR OLD
VERSION

PLAYER 1

(ASK THE OTHER PLAYER(S) TO
CHOOSE QUESTION 1 OR QUESTION 2)

A — WOULD YOU RATHER

WAKE UP IN A WORLD WITH DRAGONS

OR

A WORLD WITH DINOSAURS?

B — WOULD YOU RATHER

HAVE AN ELEPHANT'S EARS

OR

AN ELEPHANT'S TRUNK?

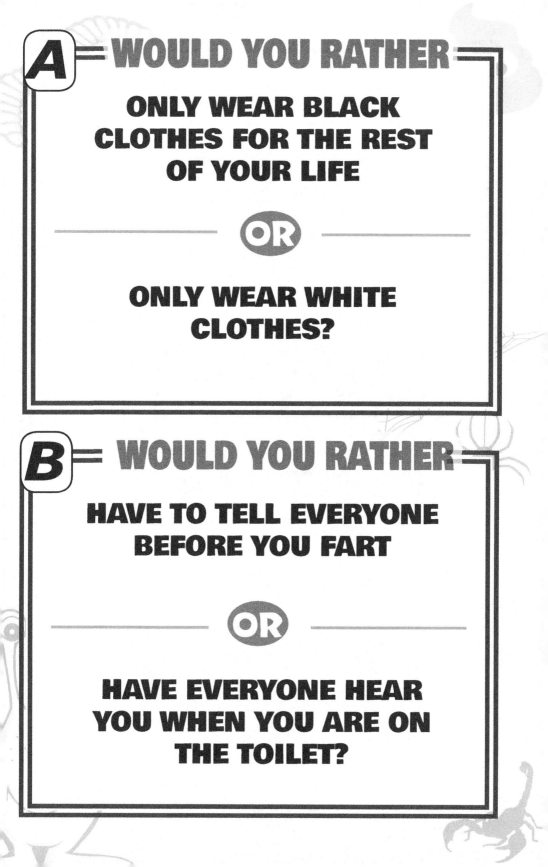

A — WOULD YOU RATHER

ONLY WEAR BLACK CLOTHES FOR THE REST OF YOUR LIFE

OR

ONLY WEAR WHITE CLOTHES?

B — WOULD YOU RATHER

HAVE TO TELL EVERYONE BEFORE YOU FART

OR

HAVE EVERYONE HEAR YOU WHEN YOU ARE ON THE TOILET?

A — WOULD YOU RATHER

BE GIVEN THE ABILITY TO FLY LIKE A BIRD, BUT YOU HAVE A BEAK LIKE A BIRD

OR

BE ABLE TO SWIM LIKE A FISH, BUT YOU HAVE GILLS?

B — WOULD YOU RATHER

LICK SOMEONE ELSE'S SHOE

OR

1. EAT AN ICE LOLLY THAT A DOG HAD LICKED?

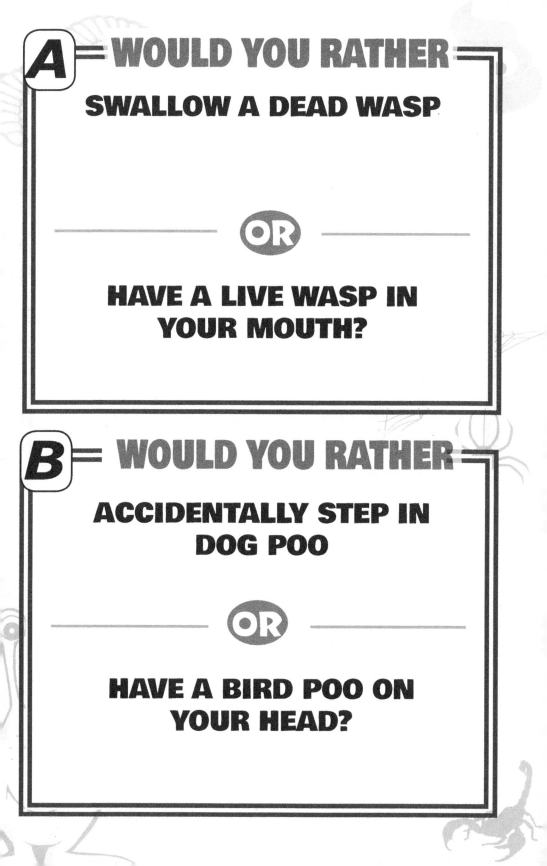

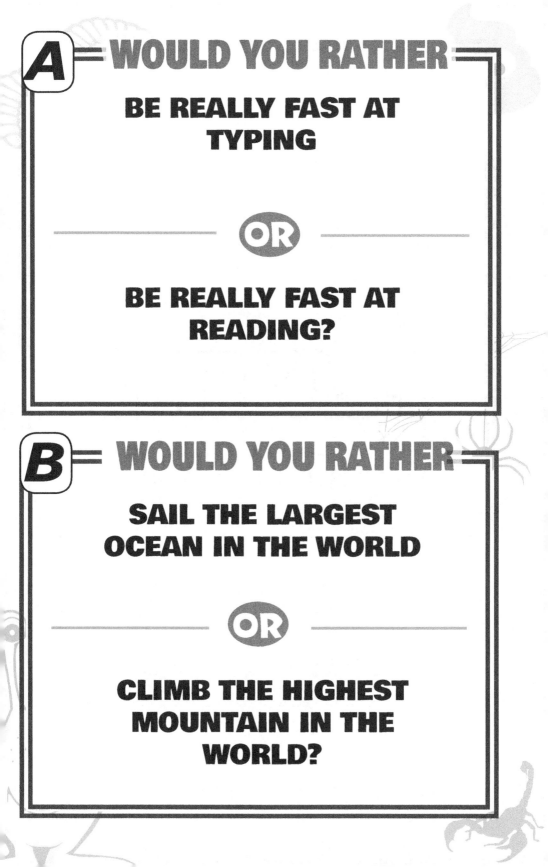

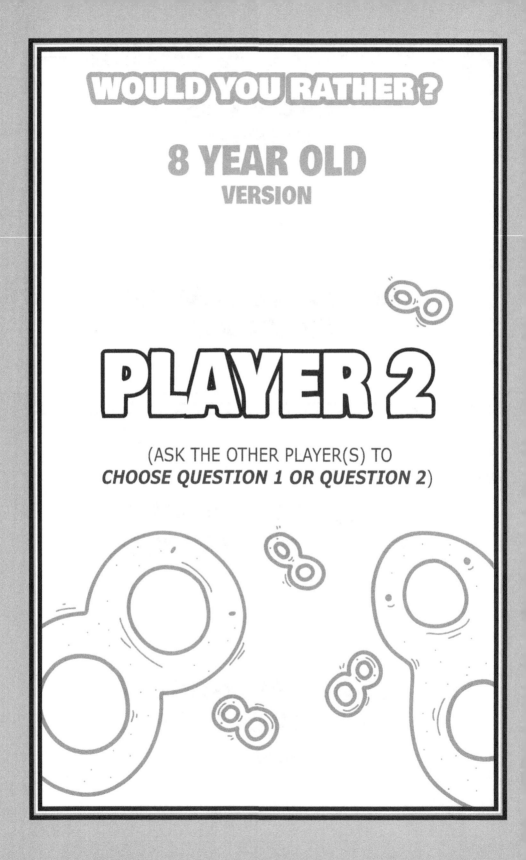

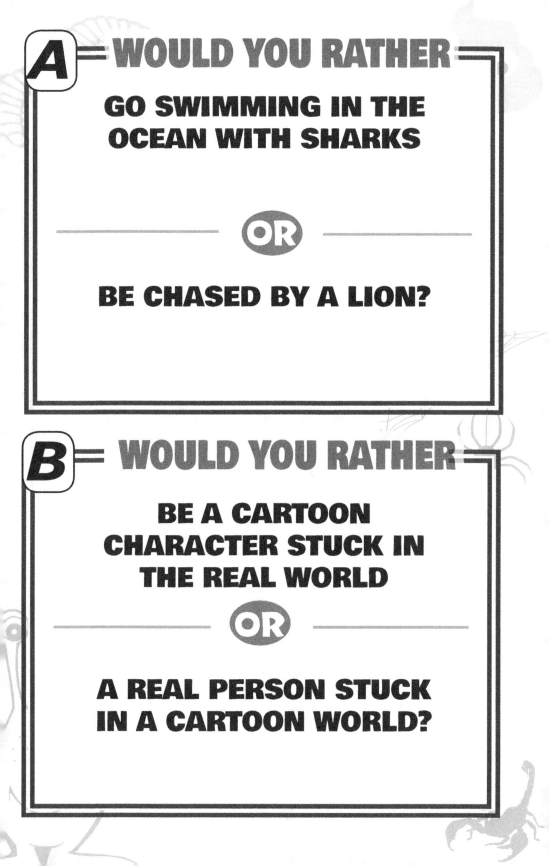

A WOULD YOU RATHER

GO SWIMMING IN THE OCEAN WITH SHARKS

OR

BE CHASED BY A LION?

B WOULD YOU RATHER

BE A CARTOON CHARACTER STUCK IN THE REAL WORLD

OR

A REAL PERSON STUCK IN A CARTOON WORLD?

WOULD YOU RATHER ?

8 YEAR OLD
VERSION

PLAYER 1

(ASK THE OTHER PLAYER(S) TO
CHOOSE QUESTION 1 OR QUESTION 2)

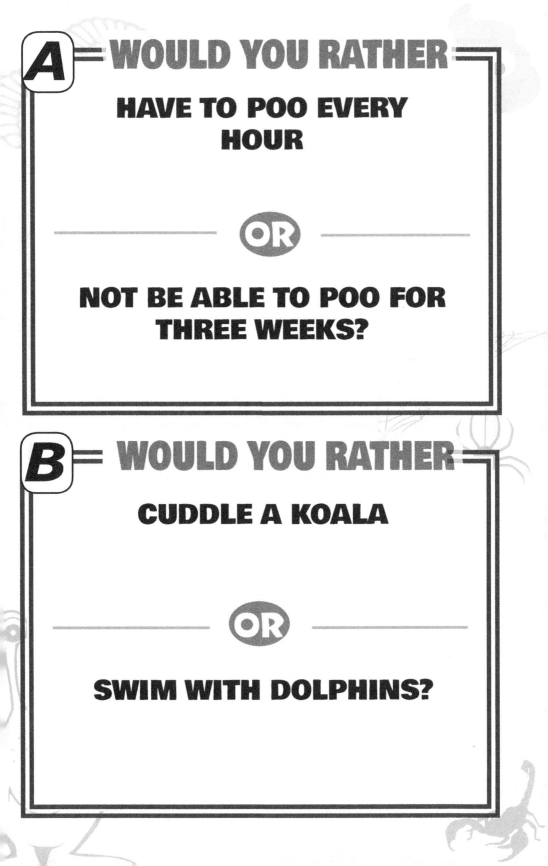

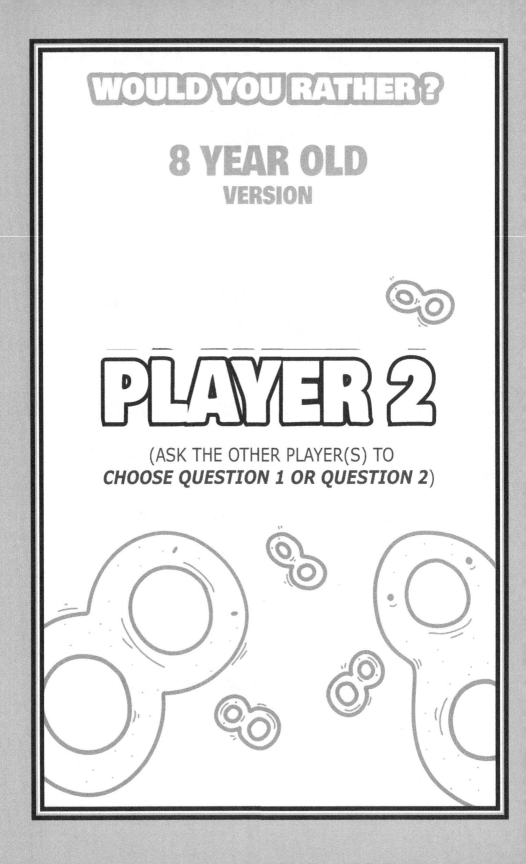

WOULD YOU RATHER ?

8 YEAR OLD
VERSION

PLAYER 2

(ASK THE OTHER PLAYER(S) TO
CHOOSE QUESTION 1 OR QUESTION 2)

A — WOULD YOU RATHER

GO FOR A JOURNEY AS A PASSENGER IN A FAST CAR

OR

1.   A STEAM TRAIN?

B — WOULD YOU RATHER

GO AWAY ON A TWO WEEK HOLIDAY IN YOUR OWN COUNTRY

OR

A WEEK ANYWHERE IN THE WORLD?

WOULD YOU RATHER?

8 YEAR OLD
VERSION

PLAYER 1

(ASK THE OTHER PLAYER(S) TO
CHOOSE QUESTION 1 OR QUESTION 2)

A = WOULD YOU RATHER

HAVE A QUIET LIFE AND NO ONE TALKS ABOUT YOU

OR

1. HAVE A BUSY LIFE AND EVERYONE GOSSIPS ABOUT YOU?

B = WOULD YOU RATHER

BE GIFTED THE POWER TO TELEPORT ANYWHERE

OR

RUN AT SUPERHUMAN SPEEDS?

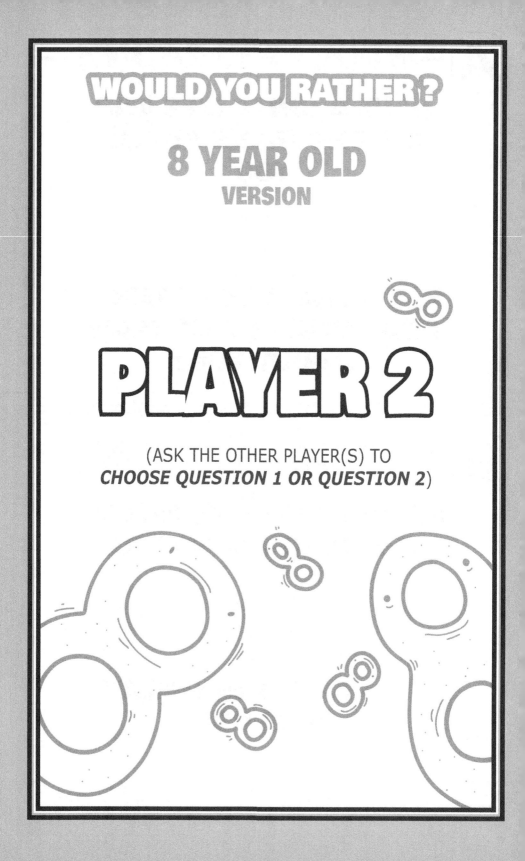

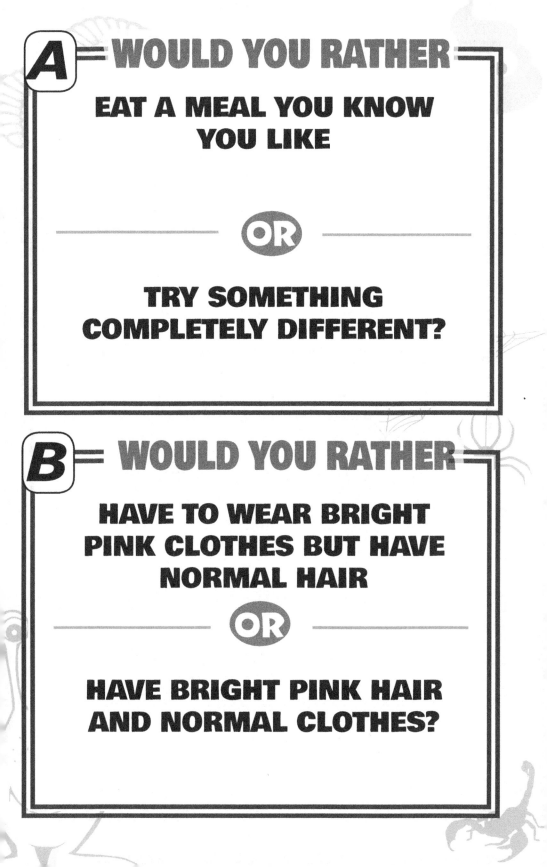

A = WOULD YOU RATHER

EAT A MEAL YOU KNOW YOU LIKE

OR

TRY SOMETHING COMPLETELY DIFFERENT?

B = WOULD YOU RATHER

HAVE TO WEAR BRIGHT PINK CLOTHES BUT HAVE NORMAL HAIR

OR

HAVE BRIGHT PINK HAIR AND NORMAL CLOTHES?

A — WOULD YOU RATHER

EAT FRUIT

OR

VEGETABLES?

B — WOULD YOU RATHER

BUY A HOUSE WITH MARSHMALLOW WALLS

OR

A HOUSE WITH COOKIE FURNITURE?

A = WOULD YOU RATHER

ONLY CELEBRATE YOUR BIRTHDAY

OR

ONLY CELEBRATE CHRISTMAS?

B = WOULD YOU RATHER

HAVE TO LIVE IN A REALLY NOISY STREET

OR

A REALLY DIRTY STREET?

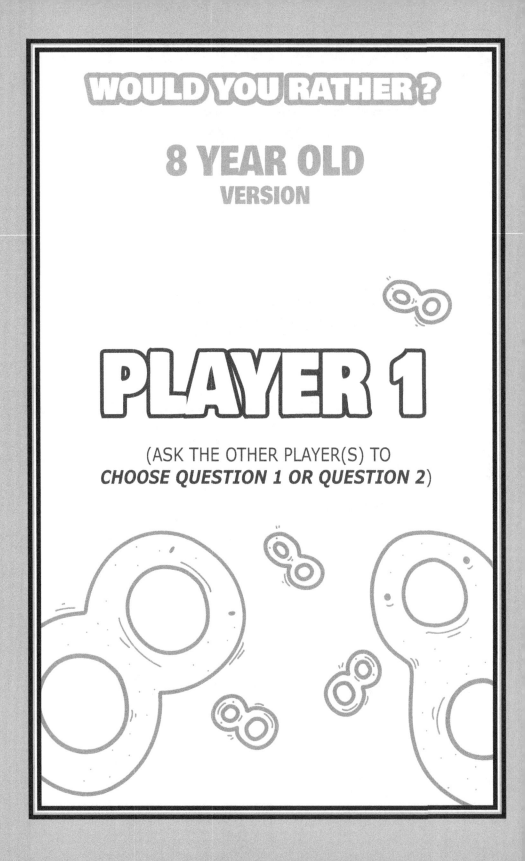

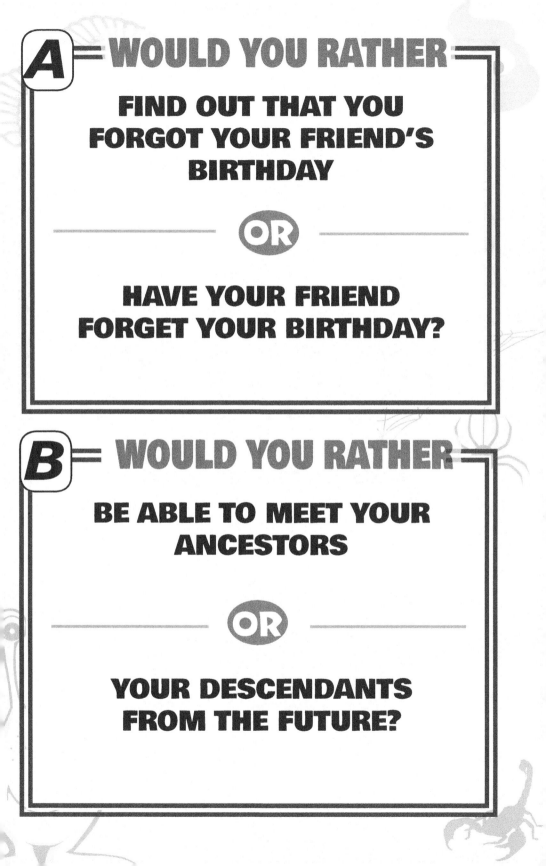

A · WOULD YOU RATHER

FIND OUT THAT YOU FORGOT YOUR FRIEND'S BIRTHDAY

OR

HAVE YOUR FRIEND FORGET YOUR BIRTHDAY?

B · WOULD YOU RATHER

BE ABLE TO MEET YOUR ANCESTORS

OR

YOUR DESCENDANTS FROM THE FUTURE?

WOULD YOU RATHER?

8 YEAR OLD
VERSION

PLAYER 2

(ASK THE OTHER PLAYER(S) TO
CHOOSE QUESTION 1 OR QUESTION 2)

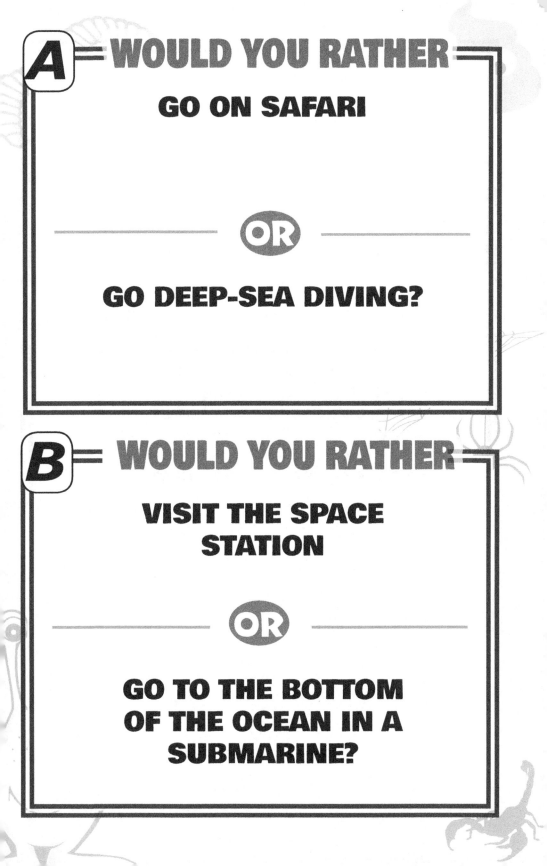

A **WOULD YOU RATHER**

GO ON SAFARI

OR

GO DEEP-SEA DIVING?

B **WOULD YOU RATHER**

VISIT THE SPACE
STATION

OR

GO TO THE BOTTOM
OF THE OCEAN IN A
SUBMARINE?

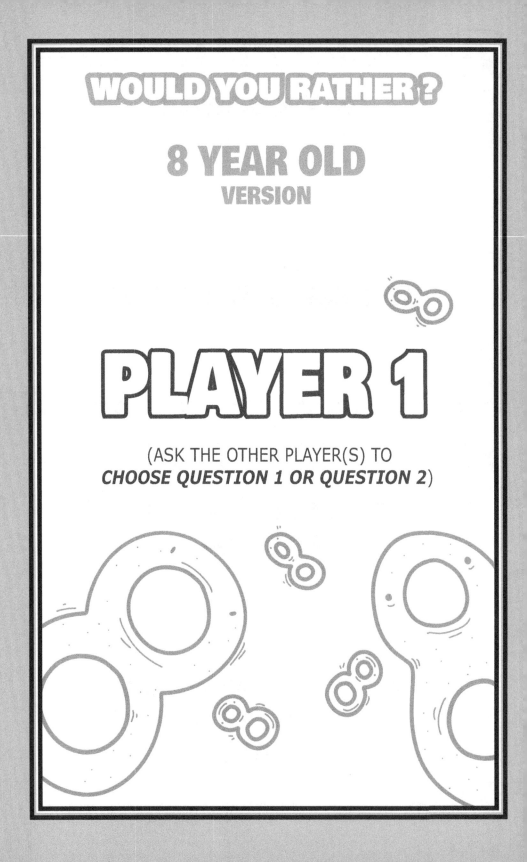

WOULD YOU RATHER ?

8 YEAR OLD
VERSION

PLAYER 1

(ASK THE OTHER PLAYER(S) TO
CHOOSE QUESTION 1 OR QUESTION 2)

A ═ WOULD YOU RATHER ═

HAVE TO SING A SONG TO YOUR CRUSH AT SCHOOL

OR

1. GIVE FLOWERS TO YOUR TEACHER?

B ═ WOULD YOU RATHER ═

EAT THE CONTENTS OF A VACUUM CLEANER

OR

EAT A PLATE OF CAT FOOD?

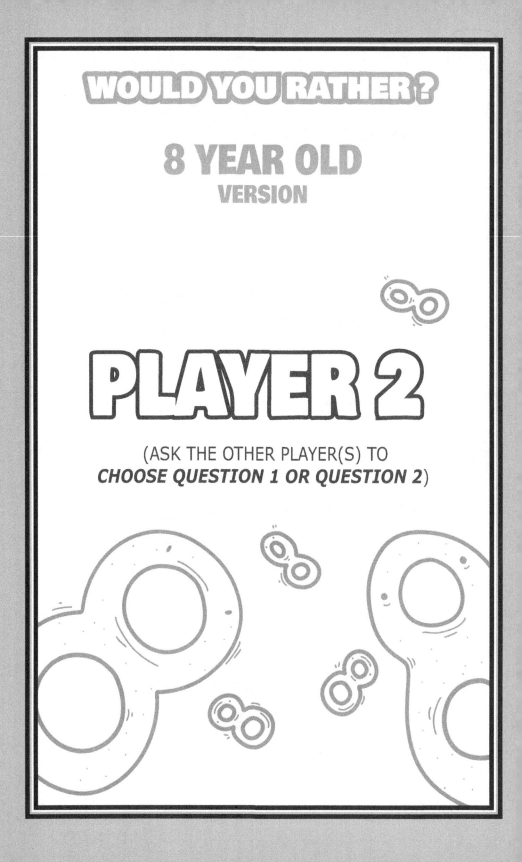

A — WOULD YOU RATHER

BE MADE TO DANCE IN FRONT OF YOUR WHOLE SCHOOL

OR

DO CHORES AT HOME EVERY NIGHT FOR A MONTH?

B — WOULD YOU RATHER

PICK FRUIT

OR

1.   SIT IN AN OFFICE?

A WOULD YOU RATHER

HAVE A LONGER HOT SUMMER

OR

A LONGER, SNOWIER WINTER?

B WOULD YOU RATHER

HAVE YOUR DAD

OR

YOUR MOM IN YOUR CLASSES AT SCHOOL?

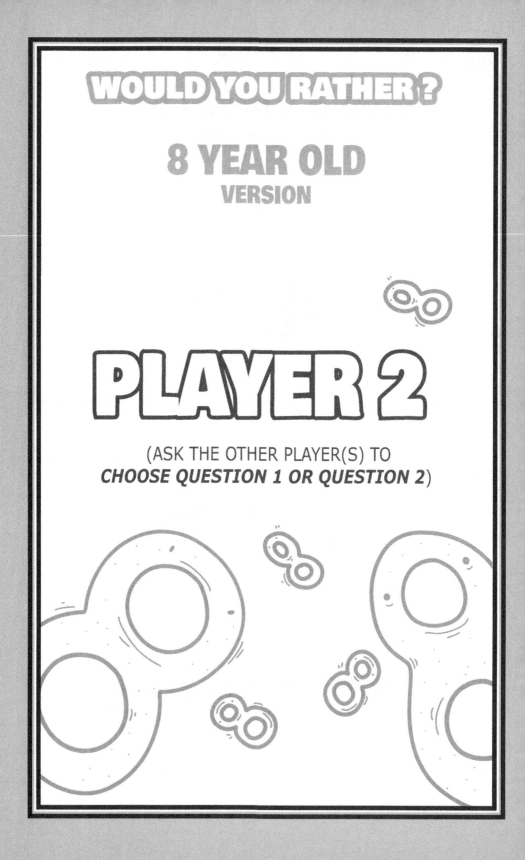

A WOULD YOU RATHER

EAT SEAWEED

OR

EAT GRASS?

B WOULD YOU RATHER

GET DRIVEN TO SCHOOL IN A RACE CAR

OR

A MONSTER TRUCK?

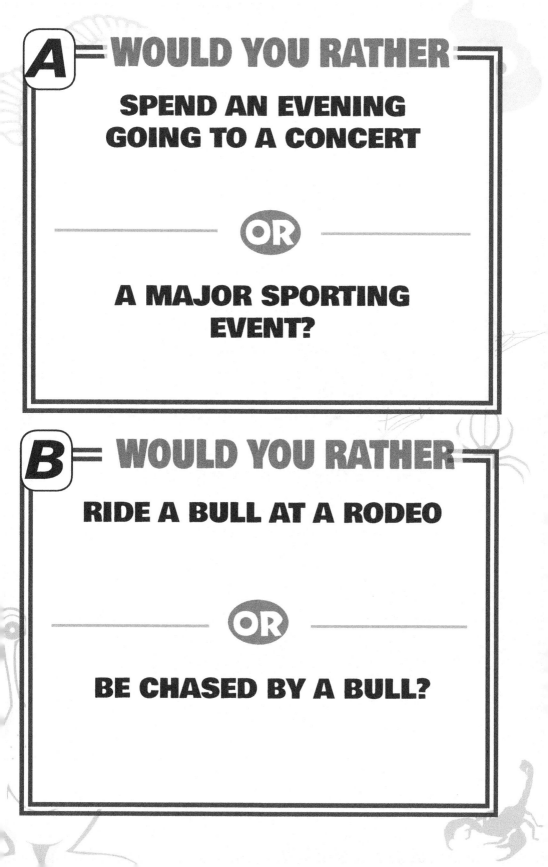

A WOULD YOU RATHER

SPEND AN EVENING GOING TO A CONCERT

OR

A MAJOR SPORTING EVENT?

B WOULD YOU RATHER

RIDE A BULL AT A RODEO

OR

BE CHASED BY A BULL?

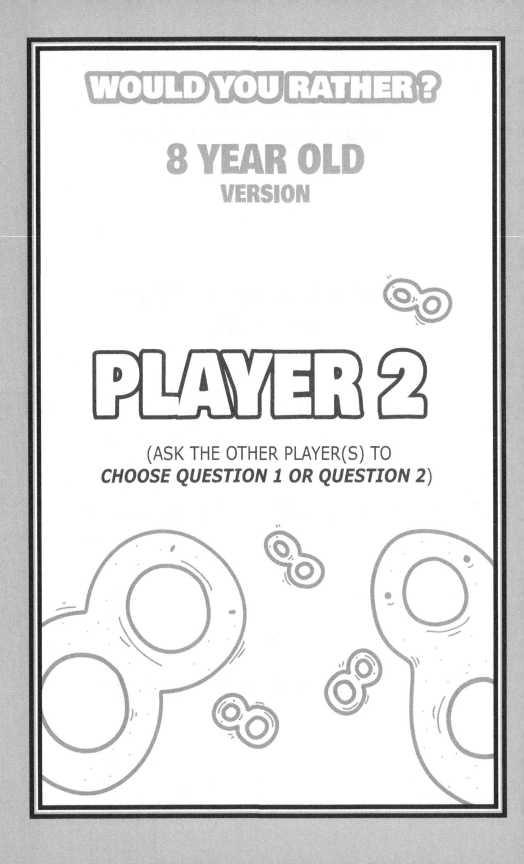

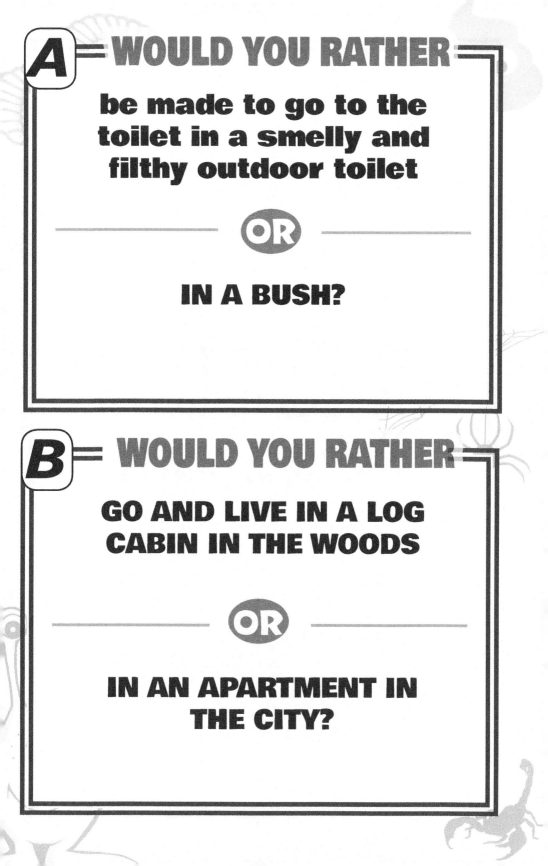

A = WOULD YOU RATHER

be made to go to the toilet in a smelly and filthy outdoor toilet

OR

IN A BUSH?

B = WOULD YOU RATHER

GO AND LIVE IN A LOG CABIN IN THE WOODS

OR

IN AN APARTMENT IN THE CITY?

A WOULD YOU RATHER

SPEND AN ENTIRE DAY AT THE ZOO

OR

GO TO A WATERPARK?

B WOULD YOU RATHER

BE FORCED TO HAVE 500 SPIDERS IN YOUR ROOM

OR

500 CRICKETS?

A | WOULD YOU RATHER

BE CURSED WITH BREATH THAT SMELLS LIKE A FART

OR

HAVE A LAUGH THAT SOUNDS LIKE A FART?

B | WOULD YOU RATHER

MARRY A RICH BUT MEAN PERSON

OR

A POOR BUT NICE PERSON?

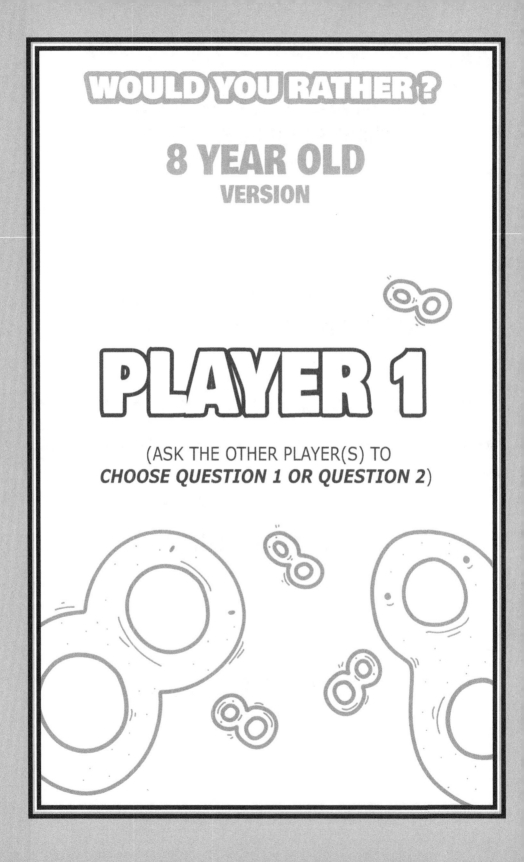

A WOULD YOU RATHER

CLIMB A HILL

OR

RUN A MILE?

B WOULD YOU RATHER

HAVE PANCAKES FOR BREAKFAST

OR

ICE CREAM FOR LUNCH?

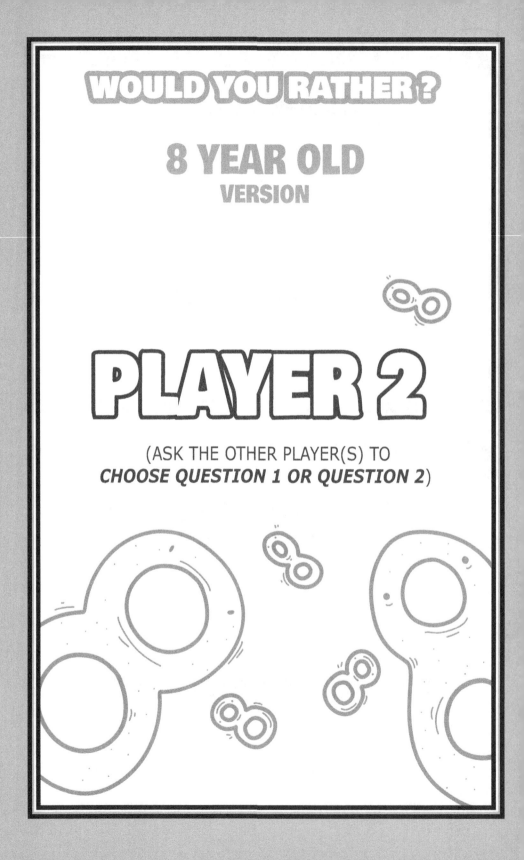

A WOULD YOU RATHER

BE GIVEN THE ABILITY TO DRAW

OR

BE ABLE TO PLAY AN INSTRUMENT?

B WOULD YOU RATHER

WATCH TV ALONE IN YOUR ROOM

OR

ON THE COUCH WITH YOUR FAMILY?

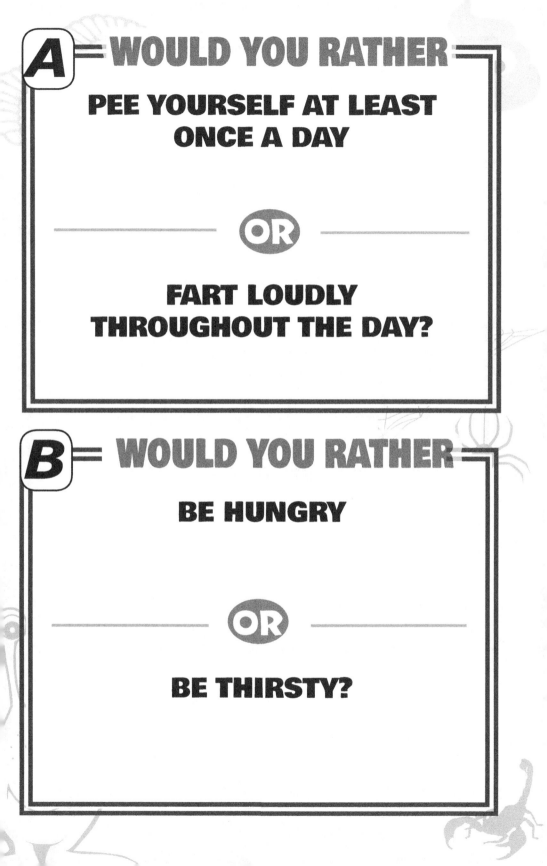

A — WOULD YOU RATHER

PEE YOURSELF AT LEAST ONCE A DAY

OR

FART LOUDLY THROUGHOUT THE DAY?

B — WOULD YOU RATHER

BE HUNGRY

OR

BE THIRSTY?

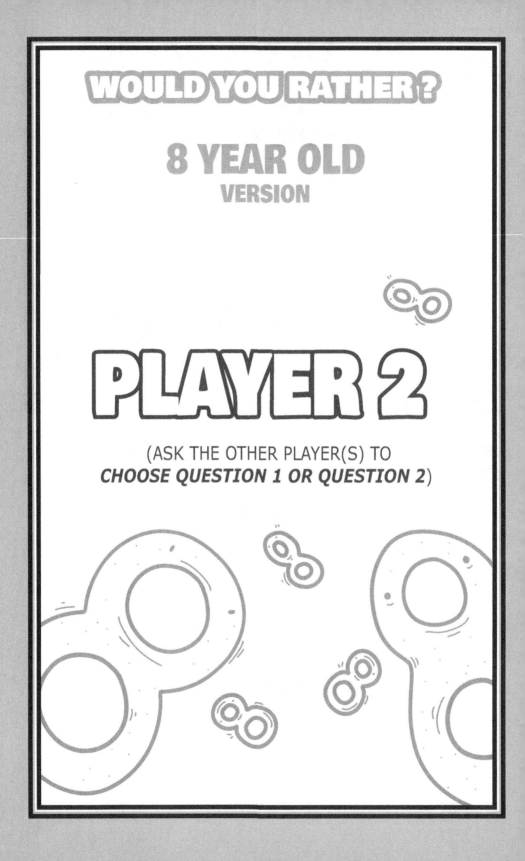

A = WOULD YOU RATHER

KNOW EVERYTHING, BUT IT'S BORING

OR

LEARN SOMETHING NEW EVERY DAY?

B = WOULD YOU RATHER

HAVE THE CHANCE OF MEETING THE EASTER BUNNY

OR

1. MEET SANTA?

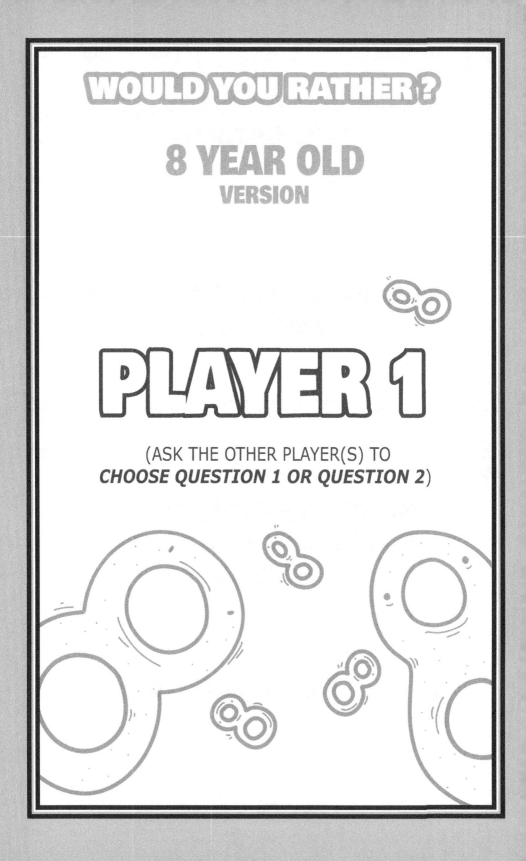

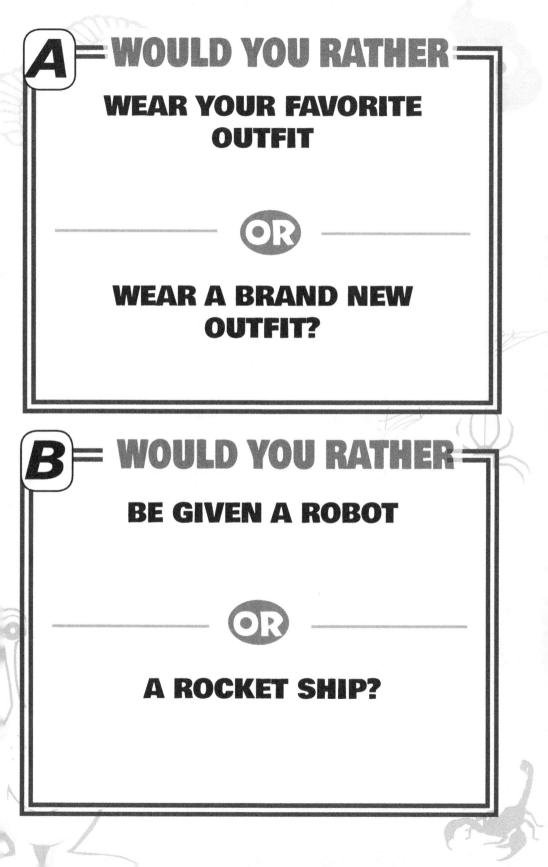

A — WOULD YOU RATHER

WEAR YOUR FAVORITE OUTFIT

OR

WEAR A BRAND NEW OUTFIT?

B — WOULD YOU RATHER

BE GIVEN A ROBOT

OR

A ROCKET SHIP?

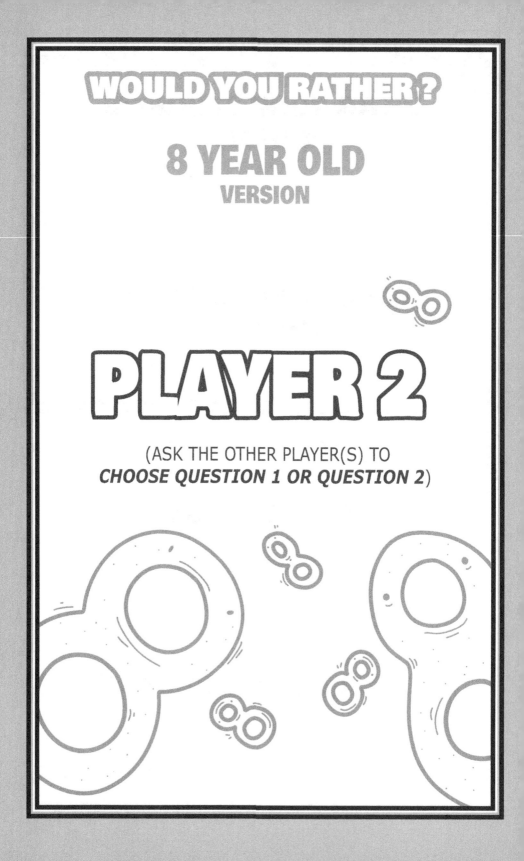

A WOULD YOU RATHER

HAVE THE ABILITY TO TURN INTO ANY BIRD

OR

ANY FISH?

B WOULD YOU RATHER

HAVE EYES LIKE A CATS

OR

COMPLETELY BLACK EYES?

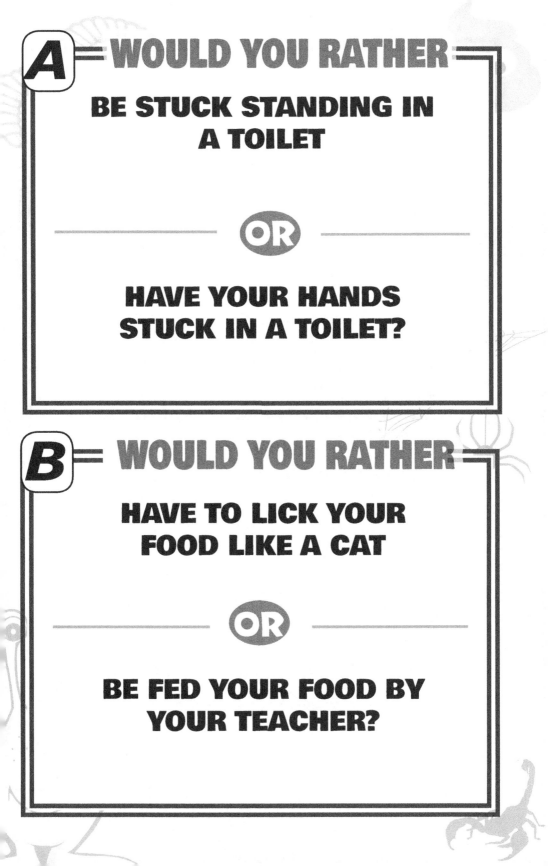

A **WOULD YOU RATHER**

BE STUCK STANDING IN
A TOILET

OR

HAVE YOUR HANDS
STUCK IN A TOILET?

B **WOULD YOU RATHER**

HAVE TO LICK YOUR
FOOD LIKE A CAT

OR

BE FED YOUR FOOD BY
YOUR TEACHER?

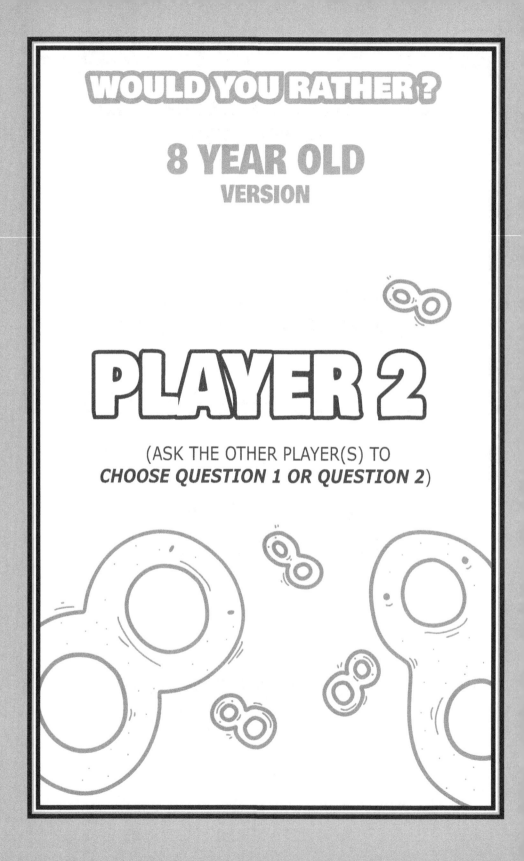

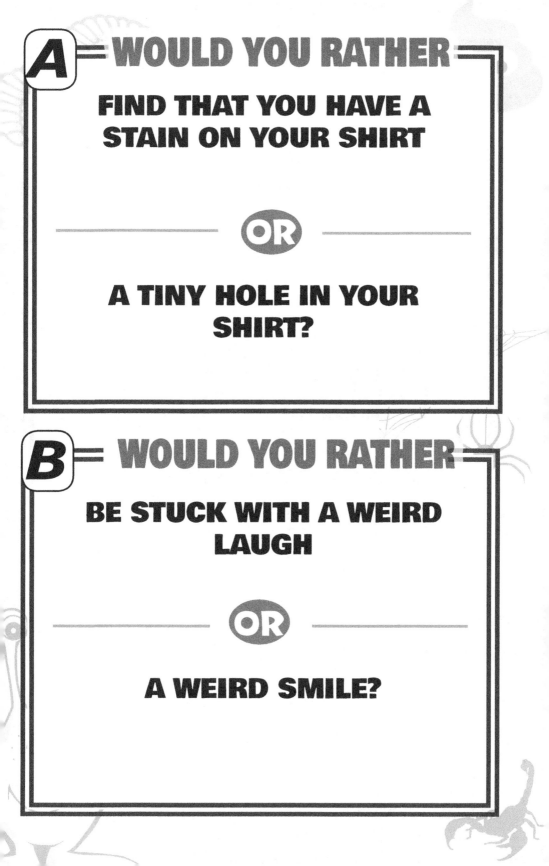

A WOULD YOU RATHER

ACCIDENTALLY FART WHEN TALKING TO SOMEONE

OR

ACCIDENTALLY SPIT IN SOMEONE'S FACE WHEN TALKING TO THEM?

B WOULD YOU RATHER

HAVE HAIR THAT CAN CHANGE COLOR

OR

HAVE HAIR THAT TASTES LIKE CANDY?

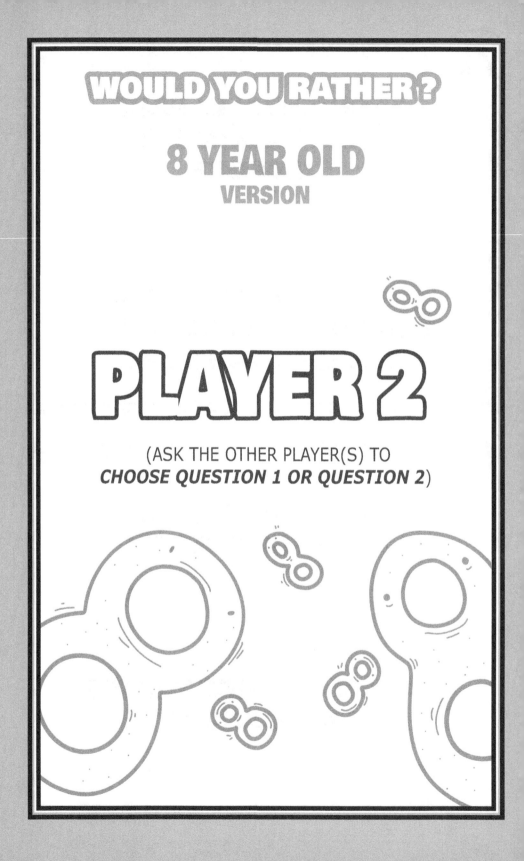

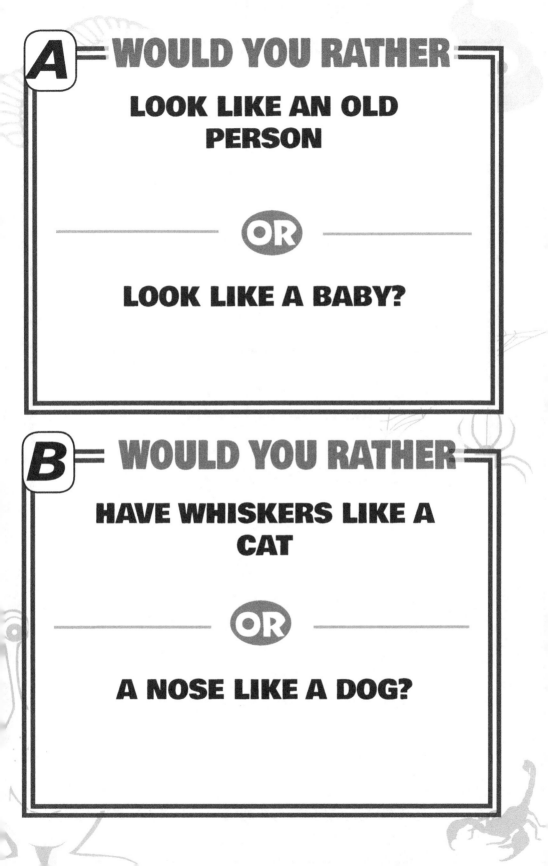

A — WOULD YOU RATHER

LOOK LIKE AN OLD PERSON

OR

LOOK LIKE A BABY?

B — WOULD YOU RATHER

HAVE WHISKERS LIKE A CAT

OR

A NOSE LIKE A DOG?

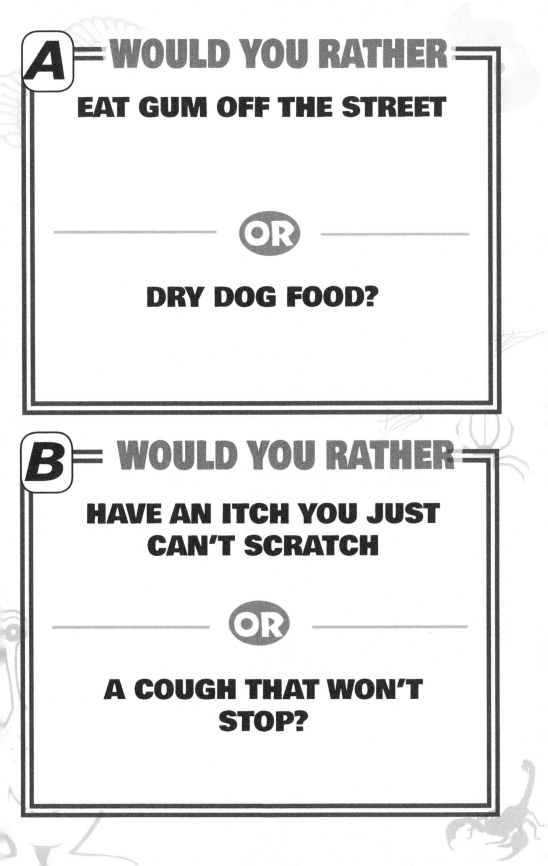

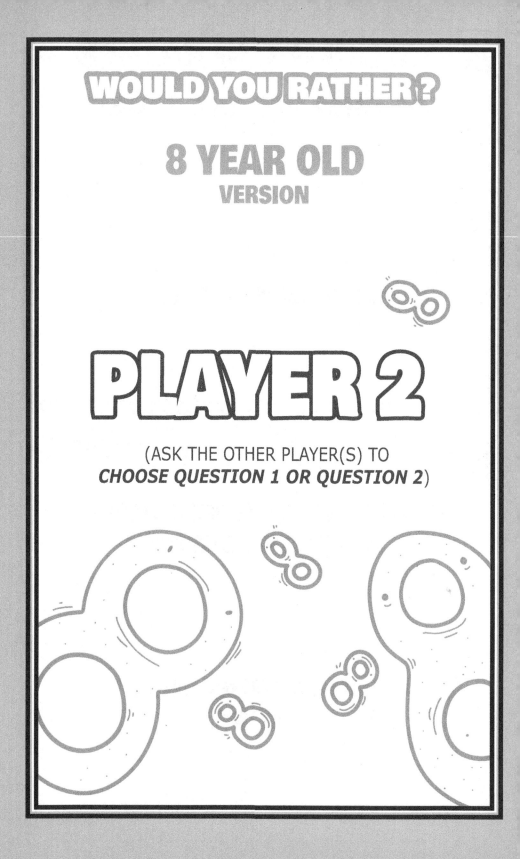

WOULD YOU RATHER?

8 YEAR OLD
VERSION

PLAYER 2

(ASK THE OTHER PLAYER(S) TO
CHOOSE QUESTION 1 OR QUESTION 2)

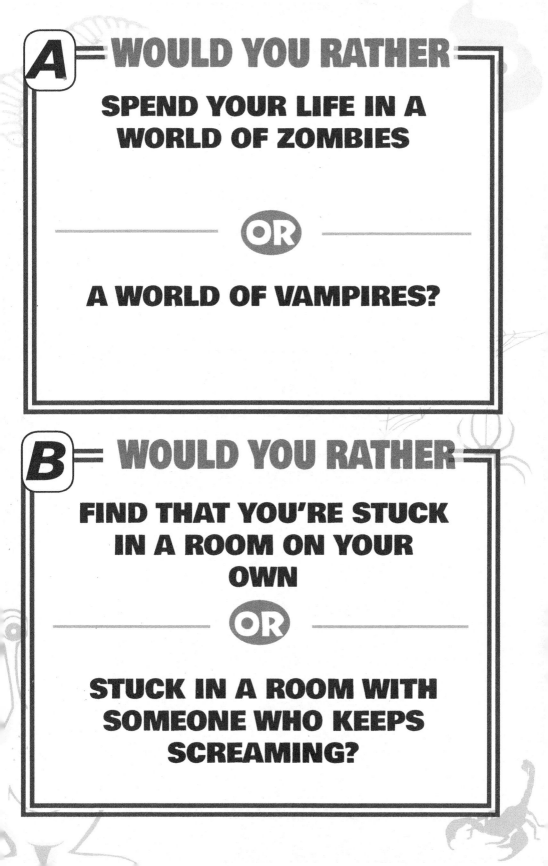

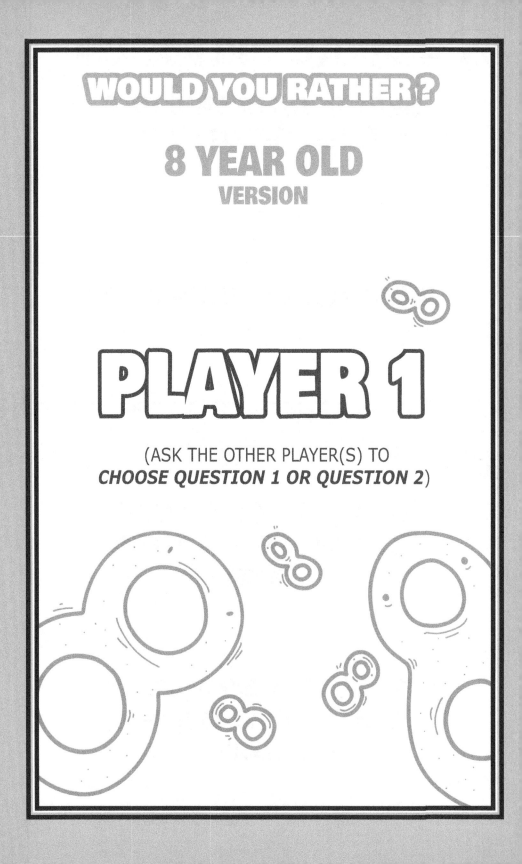

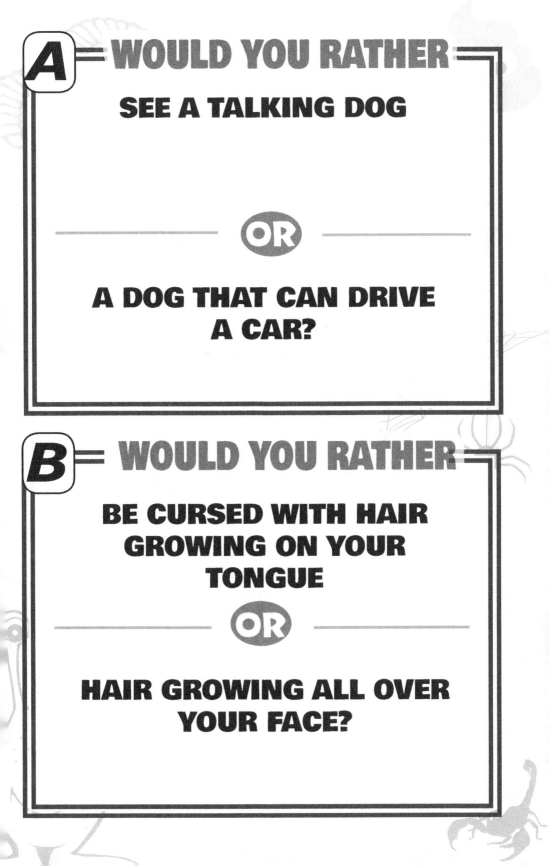

A — WOULD YOU RATHER

SEE A TALKING DOG

OR

A DOG THAT CAN DRIVE A CAR?

B — WOULD YOU RATHER

BE CURSED WITH HAIR GROWING ON YOUR TONGUE

OR

HAIR GROWING ALL OVER YOUR FACE?

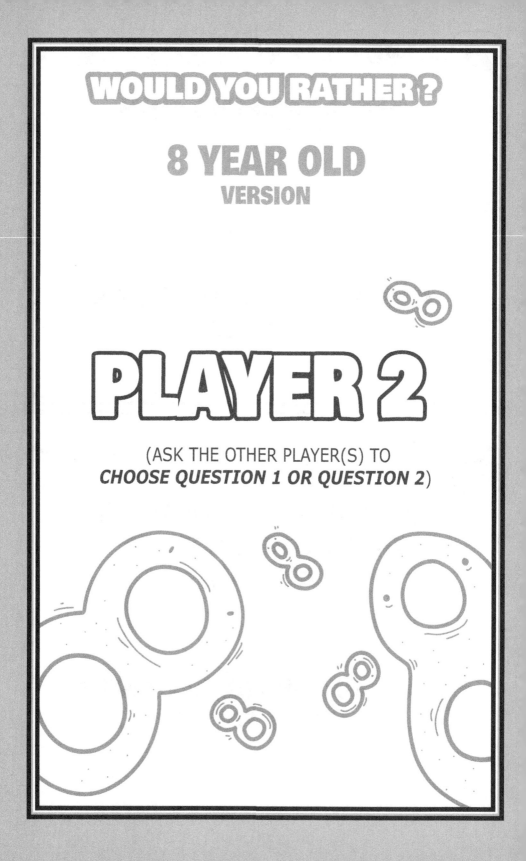

A WOULD YOU RATHER

HAVE TO RUN UP A HILL

OR

1. RUN DOWN A HILL?

B WOULD YOU RATHER

RIDE A BIKE

OR

GO SKATEBOARDING?

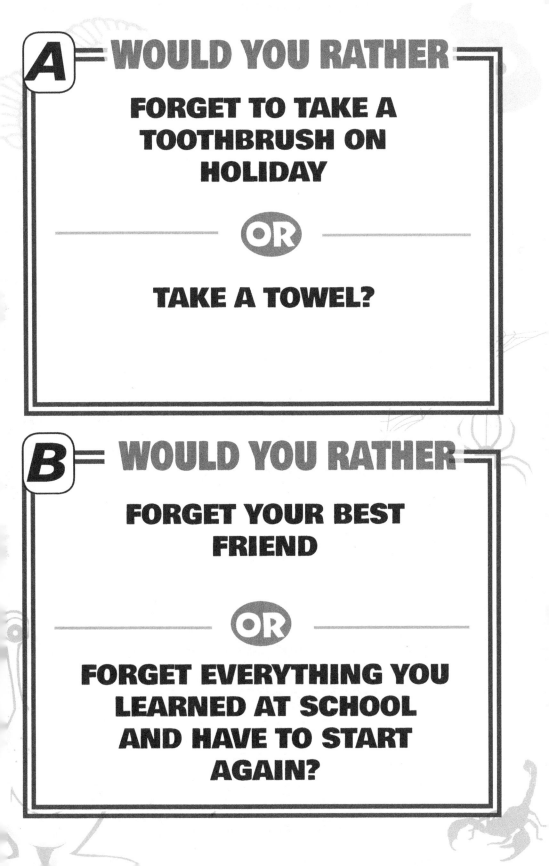

A — WOULD YOU RATHER

FORGET TO TAKE A TOOTHBRUSH ON HOLIDAY

OR

TAKE A TOWEL?

B — WOULD YOU RATHER

FORGET YOUR BEST FRIEND

OR

FORGET EVERYTHING YOU LEARNED AT SCHOOL AND HAVE TO START AGAIN?

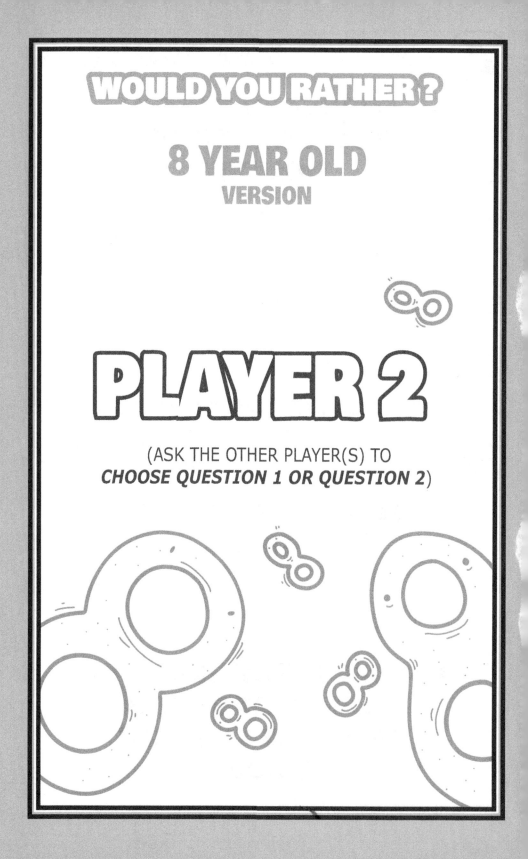